City Mou… and …y Mouse

Two More Mouse Tales from Aesop

City Mouse-Country Mouse and Two More Mouse Tales from Aesop

Pictures by John Wallner

SCHOLASTIC INC.
New York Toronto London Auckland Sydney

For Pat, my city mouse friend.
J.C.W.

Art direction by Diana Hrisinko
Type design by Emmeline Hsi

ISBN 0-590-09737-7

12 11 10 9 8 7 6 5 4 3 2 8 9/9 0 1 2 3/0

Printed in the U.S.A. 08

First Scholastic reduced format printing, September 1998

City Mouse-Country Mouse

Once upon a time a City Mouse went to visit his cousin in the country.

The Country Mouse was happy to see his cousin.

The Country Mouse did not have fine food, but he was happy to share what he had with the City Mouse.

The City Mouse turned up his nose at the country food. And he invited his cousin to have dinner with him in the city.

No sooner said than done.
The two mice set off for the city.

At last they came to the home of the City Mouse.
It was very late at night.

The City Mouse led the Country Mouse right into a grand dining room. The leftovers of a fine feast were still on the table.

Soon the two mice were eating jam and cake and all that was nice.

Suddenly they heard growling and barking.

All at once the door flew open, and in came two huge dogs. Both mice ran for their lives.

The Country Mouse made up his mind to go back to the country that very night.

What good is fine food if you can't enjoy it!
It is much better to eat plain food in peace.

The Lion and the Mouse

Once while a Lion was sleeping, a little Mouse ran up and down his back.

Soon the Lion woke up. He put his big paw on the Mouse. He opened his big jaws to swallow him.

The Mouse begged the Lion to let him go.
He promised to help the Lion some day.

The Lion laughed at the thought of a little Mouse helping a great Lion. But he lifted his paw, and he let the Mouse go.

Not long after, the Mouse saw the Lion tied to a tree.
The Lion had been trapped by some hunters.

The little Mouse went up to the great Lion and he gnawed right through the ropes. Soon the Lion was free.

"Wasn't I right?" said the little Mouse to the Lion. "Little friends can do great things."

Belling the Cat

Long ago, the mice had a meeting to talk about their enemy—the Cat. What could they do about her?

Some said this, and some said that. But at last a young mouse got up and said he had an idea.

“The Cat moves without making a sound,” he said.
“That’s why we are always in danger.”

"And," he said, "if we could hear her coming, it would be easy for us to run away."

"Now—my idea is this. We will tie a bell around the Cat's neck. Then whenever she moves, we will hear her. And we can run away!"

The mice clapped and cheered—
until an old mouse got up and said,
"That is all very well. But which one of
you is going to put the bell on the Cat?"
The mice looked at one another in silence.

And no one ever spoke again of belling the Cat.